PUFFIN BOOKS

ROAR TO THE RESCUE!

Ian Whybrow is a bestselling author of over a hundred books who is proud to have been listed as one of the top ten most-read writers in UK libraries. Among his most popular characters are the hugely successful Harry and the Bucketful of Dinosaurs, the barking mad Sniff and the much-loved Little Wolf. Ian lives in London and Herefordshire.

www.harryandthedinosaurs.co.uk

Look out for more adventures with
Harry and the Dinosaurs:
THE SNOW SMASHERS!

Harry and the Dinosaurs

Roar to the Rescue!

Ian Whybrow

Illustrated by Pedro Penizzotto

PUFFIN

PUFFIN BOOKS

Published by the Penguin Group
Penguin Books Ltd, 80 Strand, London WC2R 0RL, England
Penguin Group (USA) Inc., 375 Hudson Street, New York, New York 10014, USA
Penguin Group (Canada), 90 Eglinton Avenue East, Suite 700, Toronto, Ontario, Canada M4P 2Y3
(a division of Pearson Penguin Canada Inc.)
Penguin Ireland, 25 St Stephen's Green, Dublin 2, Ireland (a division of Penguin Books Ltd)
Penguin Group (Australia), 250 Camberwell Road, Camberwell, Victoria 3124, Australia
(a division of Pearson Australia Group Pty Ltd)
Penguin Books India Pvt Ltd, 11 Community Centre, Panchsheel Park, New Delhi – 110 017, India
Penguin Group (NZ), 67 Apollo Drive, Rosedale, North Shore 0632, New Zealand
(a division of Pearson New Zealand Ltd)
Penguin Books (South Africa) (Pty) Ltd, 24 Sturdee Avenue, Rosebank, Johannesburg 2196, South Africa

Penguin Books Ltd, Registered Offices: 80 Strand, London WC2R 0RL, England

puffinbooks.com

First published 2011
2

Text copyright © Ian Whybrow, 2011
Cover illustration copyright © Adrian Reynolds, 2011
Text illustrations copyright © Pedro Penizzotto, 2011
Character concept copyright © Ian Whybrow and Adrian Reynolds, 2011
All rights reserved

The moral right of the author and illustrators has been asserted

Set in Bembo Infant
Printed in Great Britain by Clays Ltd, St Ives plc

British Library Cataloguing in Publication Data
A CIP catalogue record for this book is available from the British Library

ISBN: 978–0–141–33274–1

www.greenpenguin.co.uk

For the Campbell children, Tom, Anna, Laura

and Sophie, with my grateful thanks for their

encouragement and advice

Chapter 1

'Hey, look! It's the kid with the bucketful of dinosaurs!'

Harry was walking across the playground towards the school gates, deep in thought. His neighbour, Mr Oakley, had been robbed at the

weekend and Harry was trying to think of a way that he and his friends could help. When he heard the shout, he froze for a second. He knew that voice. It was nasty and it belonged to Rocco Wiley.

Harry was old enough to know that if a well-known bully who's bigger and older than you starts shouting, it's best not to hang about. Besides, Harry could hear the sniggers of Rocco's mates. They were loud kids, always in trouble. One of them, Philip Wells, was called to the headteacher's office at least once a week.

Harry tried to stay calm and keep walking.

'I'm talking to you, Dino-boy!' said Rocco, louder this time. There was more laughter from his mates.

Harry stopped and turned. He saw the three boys, who were wearing identical hooded tops. They were standing with their hands in their pockets, and one boy had a foot flat against the wall.

Harry shook his head and laughed. He hoped he sounded like a person enjoying Rocco's joke and spread out his hands. 'Look, no bucket!' he called. 'And no dinosaurs. I haven't had anything to do with dinosaurs for *years*.'

'Thought you were a bit of a star, did you?' sneered Rocco. 'I bet you loved it in Assembly this morning –

showing off, everyone clapping you!'

'I had nothing to do with it,' Harry said. 'Mrs Rance was talking about ages ago! I used to be nuts about dinosaurs, that's all.'

'Yeah, right!' said Rocco. 'Like a baby playing baby games with baby toys. And I don't like that kind of stuff, do I, boys?'

'Nah! You hate baby stuff, Rocco!' agreed Philip.

Harry sighed and took another couple of steps towards the gate.

'Wait up, Dino-boy,' shouted Rocco. 'If you've grown out of baby toys then this won't worry you one bit.' He pulled a plastic dinosaur out of his pocket. It was small, and even from a distance Harry recognized it at once by the sail-shape fan on its back. It was a spinosaurus.

From his other pocket, Rocco pulled out a lighter. His friends cheered as he flicked it on and off.

Harry swallowed nervously. Lighters were dangerous and they weren't allowed at school.

Rocco grinned as a yellow flame shot up from the lighter, quite high.

His little gang of admirers looked impressed. 'Whoa!' they yelled, jumping back.

'What are you doing?' asked Harry. 'You shouldn't have that at school.'

But Rocco just laughed. Then, very slowly, he pushed the head of the tiny plastic spinosaurus into the flame.

Before he could stop himself, Harry was shouting, 'Don't!'

'Ah, diddums!' teased Rocco. 'Come and kiss it better!'

Quickly, his mates moved in to back him up. Three against one. Rocco started waving the spinosaurus about. It made the plastic start to blaze and give off lots of black smoke.

Harry couldn't stand it. 'You cowards!' he yelled, and rushed at them all.

Maybe it was the shout. Maybe it was the fierce light in Harry's eyes that scared them. Whatever it was, Rocco's mates turned and ran.

Philip Wells held his nose and started waving the back of his hand while he

retreated, as if Harry was part of the smoky stink. 'Smell you later!'

Rocco flung down the blazing dinosaur and stamped out the flames. 'All yours, Dino-boy,' he sneered, heading past Harry towards the gate.

Harry waited until he was sure he was alone before he bent down and picked up the blackened plastic dinosaur. He had risked a beating for it. Maybe that was why he wrapped it carefully in a tissue and put it in his pocket.

Chapter 2

When Harry put on his pyjamas that night, he remembered the spinosaurus. Covered in white tissue it looked like a tiny Egyptian mummy. He unwound the paper in the light of his bedside lamp. The creature was burnt and twisted by the flame, but you could still see what it was. He took it to the bathroom and ran it under warm water from the tap, straightening it and giving it a good clean-up with the wetted tissue.

When he had finished, it didn't look too

bad, though the fan on its back was ragged now. He ran his finger along the body from nose to tail, stroking the twisted ridges of the dinosaur's wounded spine. One eye had melted, he noticed. And the dinosaur had a little hole through its tail.

'Oh, grow up!' Harry whispered to himself. 'You're too old for toy dinosaurs. Put it in the bin,' he said aloud.

But he couldn't do it. Suddenly he found himself climbing on to the bathroom stool. Something made him tuck the creature out of sight in a small box of plasters on the top shelf of the wall cabinet. As he clicked the cupboard door shut, he could have sworn he heard a hiss like air from a punctured tyre.

As he headed back to bed, he thought about what had happened. It was Mrs Rance's fault. Without meaning to, she had landed him in trouble with a horrible bully!

Mrs Rance had been Harry's first teacher when he started school and she was still in charge of Reception. At Thursday Assembly, when it was Reception's turn to do something, her class had acted out a story about dinosaurs and sung a song.

But before they got started, she had pointed Harry out in the audience and made him turn bright red. 'We're going to show you some of the work we've been doing on dinosaurs,' announced Mrs Rance. 'I'm afraid we haven't got any dinosaur

experts who know quite as much as . . .'
She put her hand over her eyes and gazed
around. 'Where are you, Harry? Ah, there
you are!' When everyone in the school had
turned to stare at him, she asked, 'How
many of you can remember the wonderful
talk Harry gave when he was in my class?'

'Meeee!' cheered a couple of hundred
kids and threw their hands into the air.
Harry's friend Jack, sitting next to him on
the bench, reached round and patted him
on the back. Everyone remembered the
serious little boy standing on the stage,
clutching a seaside bucket. They had
watched as he dipped into it and started
pulling out all sorts of plastic dinosaurs.
He had introduced them all by their

names – apatosaurus . . . anchisaurus . . .
scelidosaurus – and started giving a talk.

Once he had got going on his favourite
subject, nobody could stop him! On and on
he went about what they ate for breakfast,
what armour they had, what damage they
could do, how long they were from nose
to tail, how heavy they were . . . He even
knew which ones were from the Cretaceous

period and which ones were from the Jurassic period.

In the end, the Head, Mrs Potts, had come on stage and taken his hand and gently dragged him off.

But until Rocco Wiley started giving him a hard time, Harry had pretty much stopped thinking about dinosaurs. At some point in his life, although he couldn't remember exactly *when*, it had suddenly felt very strange to be dragging a bucketful of plastic dinosaurs about with him everywhere he went. But he couldn't quite bring himself to throw them away. That was why he had decided to put the dinosaurs back where he had found them – up in the attic.

Every now and then, maybe when he

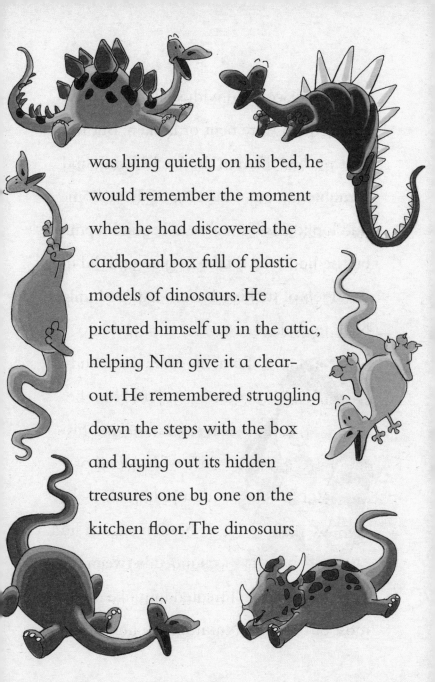

was lying quietly on his bed, he would remember the moment when he had discovered the cardboard box full of plastic models of dinosaurs. He pictured himself up in the attic, helping Nan give it a clear-out. He remembered struggling down the steps with the box and laying out its hidden treasures one by one on the kitchen floor. The dinosaurs were filthy, covered with sticky dust, and lots of them were bent or broken. But he had washed them in the kitchen sink and straightened out a number of them. Some had looked as if they were beyond repair, but he had used a tube of glue and did a good job of sticking broken legs and tails back into place.

Sam, his older sister, had come in and told him he was stupid, wasting his time with a load of dusty old junk.

Nothing much had changed between them since then. She still treated him like an idiot most of the time. Naturally, he had taken no notice of her. Instead, he'd made up his mind that the dinosaurs couldn't possibly go back into the box. He remembered explaining to Nan that they wanted to live in a bucket and how she had understood perfectly.

'That is *definitely* the right place for them,' she had agreed.

The next day, Mum had taken Harry to the library and helped him find his first book about dinosaurs. That was when the plastic models had come alive for him. Once he had found out their names, he had worked out a way of making them belong to him.

'You are my Steg-o-saur-us!' he had whispered to the little creature with the

double row of pointed plates along its back.

And then it had seemed to Harry that the dinosaur started to answer back. 'S–s–steg . . .' stammered the stegosaurus, its armoured plates rattling. And then it said, 'Oh!' and then, 'Sore!' Finally it added, 'Us.'

Once the dinosaurs knew their names, Harry had a link with them. All he had to do was say them out loud and they would

obey him. Some people have imaginary
friends; Harry had a band of loyal followers
who lived in a bucket. They joined in all his
games and would go with him wherever his
imagination led.

Harry had enjoyed all that, but these
days he was embarrassed by it. He was
older now and he had important things to
think about. Like watching out for Rocco

Wiley. Harry had hurt Rocco's pride. He and his hoodie mates would be looking for revenge.

But before Rocco had started picking on him, Harry had been trying to deal with a serious problem. He'd discovered that his neighbour, Mr Oakley, had been robbed. Harry and his friends liked mysteries and detective work. Tomorrow they were going to gather in their special meeting place and get on the case.

If we can just catch that robber and help Mr Oakley get his money back, Harry thought as he climbed into bed, *maybe Rocco will respect me a bit more. At least it'll change his mind about me still playing baby games.*

Chapter 3

After school the next day Harry was pleased to find Jack and Charlie by the bike rack, calling for him to get a move on.

'Come on, slow coach!' grinned Jack, tapping his watch and then tugging at the strap of his crash-helmet.

'What kept you?' he asked. His grey eyes twinkled. Jack didn't usually say much. He was more of a mini action-man, not scared of anyone or anything. There was nothing he couldn't do on his BMX and he was always ready to go-go-go!

Before Harry could answer him, Charlie was butting in. Shining black curls of hair punched their way out from under her helmet. She wasn't on her bike, but she had her faithful dragon skateboard tucked under her arm. She had painted the dragon on it herself. It was brilliant, all rippling gold and red.

'Hurry up!' she urged. She threw down the board. No sooner had its wheels hit the dirt than she was on the move.

In seconds, Harry had his helmet on too and was swinging on to the saddle of his bike.

Suddenly a tall, serious boy of Harry's age with chestnut-brown skin stepped in front of him. He wore glasses and his hand was raised like a policeman stopping traffic. It was Janeka Siriwardena, known to most people as Siri.

'I advise you to be careful!' said Siri, his bright eyes lighting up.

'What's up, Siri?' asked Harry. 'Aren't you coming with us?' He looked round to check that no one was listening and lowered his voice. 'Remember, we're meeting at the G.O.?'

'I haven't got my bike with me,' sighed Siri. 'My parents have been reading about road accidents. Dad thinks the roads are too dangerous for cyclists.'

'Well, where are you *meant* to ride a bike?' Jack wanted to know.

'Bad luck!' laughed Harry. 'This is what happens when you have professors for parents! Tell your dad we've all got our Cycling Proficiency certificates.'

'I did,' said Siri. 'But Dad won't listen to me.'

'You don't have to ride *your* bike,' said Charlie. 'You can ride mine instead! We can go to my house on the way and pick it up. It's just round the corner.'

'Are you sure?' he asked.

Charlie nodded. 'Of course. Mind you, you won't be able to beat me on my dragon-board!'

'We'll see about that!' said Siri, looking much happier.

'So what are we waiting for?' asked Jack,

riding circles round
them all on his
BMX. 'Let's go!'

Chapter 4

The G.O. – or Great Oak – was at least
four hundred years old, possibly more.
It was in the centre of a small wood, a
good half-mile down the lane towards
Woodseaves.

The G.O. was so wide that if four
children stood round its trunk and tried to
link hands (as Harry and his friends had
once done) they couldn't get near one
another. But if you scrambled up among
the lowest branches and removed a bit of

sacking you would find there, you could slide down into a spacious and secret room. It smelled pleasantly of dead leaves.

When Harry and Siri finally reached the wood, there was no sign of Jack's bike or Charlie's skateboard. That was good. It meant that they had followed the rules about not drawing attention to the den. Harry and Siri did the same and hid their bikes in the undergrowth. Then they pushed in among the thickets until Siri was standing with his hands against the trunk of the Great Oak. They looked up and saw Jack – way up among the top branches – waving down at them.

Siri crouched down so Harry could climb on to his shoulders. When Siri stood

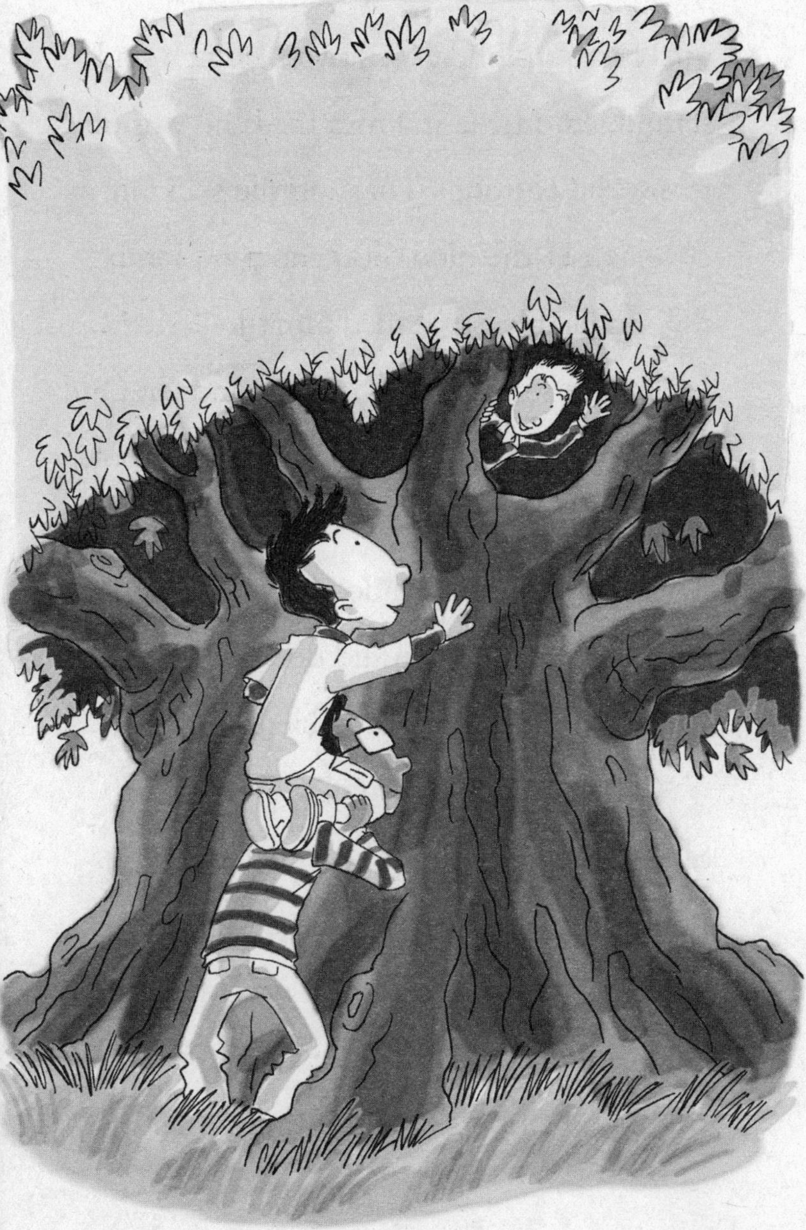

up, Harry grabbed the lowest branch and scrambled astride it. From there he was able to see the entrance. Through the sacking cover came the glow of a camping lamp.

'Ladder, please!' called Harry.

Charlie surfaced with a rope ladder. One end of it was anchored to an ancient root, deep down in the chamber, so it held fast as Siri struggled up, aided by Harry and Charlie. Silently, they slid down into the warm dark belly of the ancient tree.

'Order, order, fellow GOGOs,' panted Siri, although nobody had said anything. It was his idea that they should have a chairperson for meetings. It was also his idea to name the gang the GOGOs – they were all members of the Grand Order of the Great Oak. The others were happy to let him get on with it. As he spoke, Jack dropped down through the entrance from the higher branches above.

'Now,' said Siri seriously. 'We are gathered here because our good friend Mr Oakley has been robbed of three hundred pounds. We know that the crook was

driving a red van, which is our first clue.'

'I've got a plan!' said Charlie fiercely.
'We'll fill socks with mouldy oranges and
bash his van with them, and we won't stop
till he gives back the money.'

'But nobody even knows where he is,'
Jack pointed out. 'Not even the police!'

'Hmm, socks filled with mouldy oranges,' murmured Siri. 'That is most imaginative, Charlie, but . . .'

'Yes, they would be excellent because they wouldn't do any *serious* damage,' she explained. 'And best of all, the police could easily trace Red Van Man if he was sticky all over!'

Harry was grateful to Charlie for wanting to help. 'Perhaps we should go over the facts of the case?' he said. 'It may help us all.'

'Good idea, Harry,' replied Siri. 'Tell us again what happened.'

Chapter 5

So Harry went over what had happened. Everyone knew and liked Mr Oakley. He was Harry's nearest neighbour and he owned the farm just along the lane from where Harry and his family lived. When Harry's dad had died, before Harry was two, Mr Oakley had made it his business to keep an eye on the family. It was hard to believe that anyone would take advantage of such a nice person.

At the weekend, Mr Oakley had come

over to Harry's house while the whole family was out and started tidying up the hedges with his hedge-trimmer. While he was working, a red van pulled up and the driver got out and started unloading furniture on to Harry's drive. Mr Oakley stopped his machine and asked what was going on.

'The man said he was delivering some "antiques" for the lady of the house,' explained Harry. '"They're wanted urgent" were his exact words to Mr Oakley. "And I need folding money for them."' The words 'folding money' were new to Harry, which was why he remembered them. 'Unless he was paid in cash, the man said, he had orders to take everything back to the shop.'

Charlie, Jack and Siri stayed silent, listening carefully to Harry's story.

Mr Oakley hadn't wanted Harry's mum to be disappointed. Because that day was market-day and he had just sold some sheep, he happened to be carrying £300 in cash. So he paid the man and helped him put the furniture into the garage. There was a big dining table and a set of chairs.

When Mr Oakley asked for a receipt, the man told him that 'the lady' already had one. But then he gave him a business card for a shop called Bygones in Stapleton, a village ten miles away. On the back of the card, the name  'Barry' was written in pencil.

'Then he thanked Mr Oakley and drove off in the red van,' concluded Harry.

'And your mum said she'd never ordered any furniture?' asked Siri.

Harry nodded. 'That's right. And, as soon as Mum saw it, she could see that it was just a load of old woodwormy junk, not proper antiques at all.'

'What a dirty trick!' said Jack, disgusted, waving the lamp and making their shadows dance on the walls.

'A crook, that's what he is!' added Charlie. 'What did he look like?'

'Middle-aged. Greasy white hair combed straight back. Work clothes. That's it,' said Harry.

Siri stroked his chin. 'Hmm. Did Mr Oakley take the number plate of the van?' he asked.

'No, he didn't know anything was wrong until we got home,' said Harry. 'But he did phone the number on the card and ask for Barry.'

'And what happened?' asked Charlie.

'A lady answered. She said her husband's name was Barry, but he didn't own a red van, they didn't have an assistant and they didn't sell furniture. Bygones only sells small stuff – plates and books, bits of silver, things like that,' explained Harry. 'She had no idea how the man had got hold of her husband's card.'

'...And when your nan heard that, she called the police,' added Siri.

'Yes. But the policeman who came to see us had bad news,' said Harry. 'He told us if the police ever catch up with Red Van Man, he can just say that he sold the furniture to Mr Oakley. There's nobody else who can prove that things happened the way Mr Oakley says they did.'

'So your mum's lost three hundred pounds? Wow!' breathed Jack. 'I could buy a brilliant BMX for that.'

'Mum's OK. It's Mr Oakley who got robbed,' sighed Harry. 'He won't let Mum pay him back. He says it serves him right for being a silly old fool.'

'That's not true!' said Charlie, feeling sorry for him.

'We must find Red Van Man and force

him to pay for his crime!' added Siri.

'Yeah, but how?' asked Jack.

'We make our own investigation and solve this mystery!' said Siri, thumping his knee with his fist. 'The place to begin is Bygones of Stapleton. I'm sure we'll find a clue there. Let's go, GOGOs!' He stood up with excitement. *Clunk*. Then he sat down again, holding his head. He'd forgotten how low the ceiling was.

Ouch.

'I agree,' said Harry. 'Tomorrow is Saturday so let's go then and see what we can find.'

Chapter 6

'No, Mr Oakley – don't give him your money!'

Harry sat up in bed and felt for the switch on his bedside lamp. Light! That's what you need to get rid of a nightmare. He'd had a horrible dream where he was trying to save Mr Oakley from being robbed. But all that happened was that Red Van Man knocked him to the ground, then got in his car and drove away again. Harry could still hear the sound of him revving the engine.

Where was that switch? He felt around, scattering a pile of books. He almost knocked over a glass of water. Something wasn't quite right. This was definitely his room and he was sure he was awake. He was in his own bed – yet the shocking rip-roar of the van's revving engine did not stop.

VRRROOOOOM – VAAAH!
VRRROOOOOM – VAAAH!

The noise rattled the windows and made the air in the room seem to vibrate. At last he found the switch and flicked the lamp on.

What Harry saw knocked the breath out of him. A *thing* – scaly and covered with

flaky greenish skin – filled the room. In fact,
part of it spilled out through the open door
into the corridor! It lay there like some
huge crocodile, but with something that
looked like a flapping broken fence stuck
on to its back. Slowly, back and forth, it was
scraping the side of its long evil jaw against

the wardrobe like a saw. The thing had its
eye closed and was groaning. That was the
sound Harry could hear, not the engine from
his nightmare. Now and then its great jaws
snapped together like a trap.

As Harry ducked under his duvet, pulling
it around his ears for protection, the thing
turned its long snout towards him. He heard

its breath hissing as its nostrils winked open
and closed, sniffing him.

Fsssss! Fsssss!

The gust of air from its nostrils sent the
curtains flapping. Harry risked taking a peek
out from under the duvet. For a moment the
creature glowed like molten rock and then
cooled to the colour of oily mud.

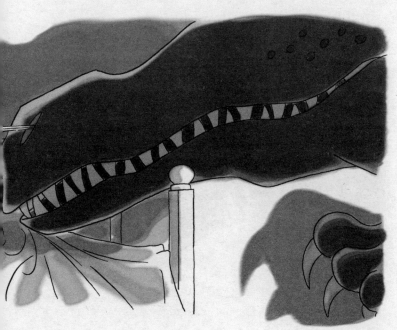

Harry gasped, his heart pounding as he expected to be gulped down like a meatball. Then he saw something that set his mind whirling. As the other side of the long flat head swung towards him, Harry saw that its skull was worn smooth. It was missing an eye!

'Spinosaurus?' whispered Harry. *I must still be dreaming*, he thought.

'Ahhhhh!' rumbled the monster in a deep voice. Its one good eye was half-closed and its clusters of ragged teeth formed into a kind of smile. 'Sorry to scare you. That side of my face keeps itching.' The beast turned his good eye on the boy again. 'Nice to see you again, Harry. Three-Horned Face said you would be in touch eventually. What took you so long?'

Harry's mouth dropped open. 'Three-Horned Face? You mean Triceratops?'

'The very same,' grinned the monster.

'But I left all my dinosaurs in the bucket in the attic,' Harry whispered. 'I've grown out of them. I've finished with them.'

'Oh no,' said Spinosaurus. 'Humans don't *finish* with dinosaurs, not once they get to know us. If we like somebody, we back you up. We never go away. B.U.Ds stick around.'

'Buds?' asked Harry.

'B-U-Ds. Back-Up Dinosaurs,' said Spinosaurus.

'But it's been ages!'

'Ah, you can lose touch with us for a while; that's normal. But B.U.Ds are always around. We're patient. We go back millions of years, remember. We can wait. Then we come back at just the right moment.'

'Are you the spinosaurus I picked up the other day?' asked Harry, still amazed.

'It took courage to try to protect me,' said the creature. 'Now all the dinosaurs are yours to command.' His crocodile jaws formed into a sort-of smile.

'All the dinosaurs?' said Harry.

'Yes, B.U.Ds are everywhere, really. We're hidden, that's all. We can fit into any space. The important thing is . . . you have to believe in us. That's hard for a lot of people. But not for you, Harry.'

'You mean you came to me because I couldn't bring myself to throw you away?' gasped Harry.

'That's it! Deep down, we matter to you. That's why you cleaned me up and put me in a safe place after I had been attacked.' With a hiss, Spinosaurus ran the back of a clawed front paw over his melted face. 'You don't believe in us in the old way, of course. That's because we're not quite the same as we were when you were younger. These days we're a lot *scarier*, I think you'll agree.'

In a flash, he gave a terrifying grunt, pulled himself up on his mighty hind legs, lit up for a moment like a giant neon sign and snapped his bony jaws. He hooked his long scaly snout under the duvet and tossed it into the air! Then he smiled. 'We've grown up too, you see?'

'D-do you mean you've become full-size?' stammered Harry, who was now sitting on a bare

mattress. He wondered what Rocco
and his friends would think if he brought
a real dinosaur
to school.

'Sometimes we're full-size, yes,' the creature replied, stretching out again and making himself less scary. 'As a matter of fact, I'm only half-size at the moment. But to make things easy for you, from now on, if you need to call on one of us for back-up – just check on your key-ring. But only for problems you really can't tackle on your own. Understand?'

Suddenly there were footsteps in the hallway. Mum rushed into the room in her nightie and snapped the main bedroom light on.

Chapter 7

'Harry!' Mum gasped, looking from Harry sitting up in bed to the duvet on the floor. 'What's the matter? Did you have a nightmare?'

She felt his forehead. 'You're dreadfully hot. Wait, I'll get an aspirin.'

'No, it's OK, Mum. I fell out of bed, that's all.' Harry was relieved – and amazed – to see that Spinosaurus had completely disappeared.

Mum carried on fussing anyway. She

tucked Harry under the duvet as if he was still a little boy. Then she clicked off the lights before she closed the door.

Harry counted to a hundred before he reached out and turned on his bedside lamp. There was no sign of the dinosaur.

With a creak, the wardrobe door opened by itself. Harry pulled the duvet over his ears again. A snout with winking nostrils appeared.

Fssssss.

Then, like a telescope slowly clicking out, section by section, Spinosaurus expanded himself. He sat up on his back legs. This time, even fully formed, he was no bigger than a large dog. For the first time, Harry noticed the tip of his tail. It

had a hole clean through it.

'As I was saying,' rumbled the beast, moving its snapping snout closer, 'we fit into any space and we're scarier than we were . . . A bit more . . . *real*, you might say. *Fssssss!* But don't worry. We are also invisible to other people. We are solid, but we leave no footprints. But if you wish, you can command us to show ourselves.' He gave a sudden hop and jumped in front of Harry's full-length mirror. There was no reflection.

Harry suddenly felt very tired. 'So you came because . . .'

'You got in touch. You stroked me nose-to-tail. If you want a B.U.D. pocket-size and plasticated, you must run your hand along it the other way. Remember that.'

'P-pocket-size? Plasticated?' stammered Harry.

'Some creatures hibernate,' explained Spinosaurus. 'Special dinosaurs like us prefer to plasticate.'

Harry covered his mouth to stifle a yawn.

His eyes were feeling heavy. 'So the others are out there, waiting to back me up if I need them? Triceratops, Anchisaurus . . . all of them?' He yawned again. 'I think I need to sleep. Can we talk again in the morning?'

'Certainly. As you wish. We are at your service.'

'Where are the others now, exactly?' asked Harry. 'In the attic?'

'Let's just say they're waiting for you to get in touch . . .' said the dinosaur. 'They can sense when you have a problem. They will decide which of them can best help. If you need them, you know the drill: check on your key-ring. Now put your hand out.'

Harry let his arm hang over the side of the bed. It crossed his mind that even a small spinosaurus could snap it off at the elbow. Instead it rubbed against him like a cat. The skin was as rough as tree-bark, not at all slimy, and surprisingly warm. Slowly the creature moved himself backwards against Harry's trailing fingers, tail-to-nose.

Then suddenly it was gone.

'Where are you?' whispered Harry.

He sat up urgently and grabbed his jeans
that were hanging over the back of his
chair. He needed to check something. *If you
want us pocket-size . . .*

When he reached into the right front
pocket, his fingers found his keys. There
was something new on his key-ring. It was
a collection of small, thin plastic cards.
When he held them up to the light, they
shone all colours, like patches of oil. He
flipped through them, looking for pictures
or writing, but they were blank. Without
warning, one of them started to feel warm.
It began to glow. Suddenly Harry could
make out a shape forming on it. There! The

spinosaurus! It was on the card, swinging by
its tail from his key-ring! Harry tipped the
card away from him to get a better look.
The spinosaurus turned his snout towards
the boy and his good eye winked at him.
Harry placed his thumb on the glowing
body of the creature.

'So if I need you, I just run my thumb along your body, nose-to-tail,' he muttered sleepily. The eye winked again.

Harry let himself fall backwards and was asleep almost before his head hit the pillow. A split second before things went black, two words formed in his mind:

B.U.D.

Plasticated.

Chapter 8

By ten o'clock the following morning, the GOGOs were on their mission. Harry still couldn't believe what had happened in the middle of the night, but he reached into his pocket and checked his key-ring for the little collection of cards. Good. They were there.

It was a fabulous sunny day. The sky was blue, birds sang their heads off – and nobody noticed. Harry and his friends were all too busy pedalling fast along the country

lanes towards Stapleton. (All except Charlie, who preferred to rumble along on her trusty dragon-board. When she needed a tow, Jack was happy to let her hang on to the back of his BMX.) Siri was riding an old-fashioned bike with the world's clankiest mudguards.

'So it worked,' laughed Harry. 'You got your bike out of jail! What did you say to your parents?'

'Simple,' puffed Siri. 'I reminded them that I had to exercise to stay healthy.'

'Yeah, right!' said Charlie. 'So where are you supposed to be today? Did you tell them a naughty lie?'

'Not exactly,' replied Siri, looking a bit ashamed. 'I told them the truth. I am helping Mr Oakley.'

'Me too!' Jack, Charlie and Harry laughed together.

They pushed on, encouraging one another on the steep hills and *wahoo*-ing as they went down the other side. There was no traffic to speak of. In an hour they saw no more than six cars and a tractor.

They came to a cattle grid and everyone slowed down.

'Time for lunch!' said Siri, braking hard and getting off his bike. 'I trust you have all brought lashings of ginger beer!'

'Who do you think we are, the Famous Four or something?' yelled Harry, with a hoot of laughter. He raised a cloud of dust with a wheelie. 'We're the GOGOs! We all *hate* ginger beer.'

'Oh dear,' said Siri. 'Then I suppose you will also hate my mother's amazing samosas and onion bhajis. I will have to eat all twenty of them myself!'

'Whoa! Yes, please!' squealed Charlie. 'They're delicious. Swap you a cheese and pickle sandwich for two of each!'

While the others bumped their wheels over the metal poles of the cattle grid, Jack could not resist the chance to test the stunt pegs on his bike.

'Watch this!' he called as his friends got their picnic ready on the grass.

Alongside the grid a low iron railing was fixed. Jack checked his helmet was strapped on tight. Then he rode twenty metres back the way they'd come, turned and pedalled fast to get up

plenty of speed. With his blond hair flying, he flipped up both wheels. He performed an ear-splitting grind along the rail and cleared the cattle grid with barely a couple of centimetres to spare.

Wow! His friends were amazed. 'I'm glad my parents aren't here to see you do that,' said Siri.

As Jack got high-fives all round, Charlie gave him a double helping of chocolate brownies.

Ten minutes later they were all off again and racing. They didn't pause for breath until they reached the centre of Stapleton. It wasn't exactly busy: there was just the village store and the shop next to it – Bygones. The four children parked their bikes and skateboard outside. It was time for the investigation to begin.

Chapter 9

An old-fashioned bell jingled as the children piled through the door of Bygones and gazed at the shelves loaded with secondhand books, china, glass, jewellery and all sorts of other treasures. Every inch of the walls was covered with old paintings.

A cheery man wearing a bright checked shirt with a fancy silk scarf welcomed them. He had a monocle in his left eye. He ran his thumbs along his bushy moustache. 'What can I do for you?' asked the

shopkeeper, slapping his hands together.

'Are you Barry, by any chance?' asked
Harry.

The man looked so surprised that his
monocle slipped from his eye and dangled
on its string. He snapped his fingers. 'Ah!
Now you're not the first person to ask my
name, you know. Are you anything to do
with the man who phoned my wife about
our business card?' he said.

The children nodded.

'Well!' the man went on. 'Barry it is. And I'll tell you what I told my wife just this morning. I couldn't think at the time who I gave my card to, but it came back to me later. It was a very nice chap in a van. He stopped by the shop a couple of weeks ago to ask if we needed any odd jobs doing – gardening, decorating, clearing old furniture . . . that sort of thing. I said we had a rotten old table and some chairs that needed taking to the dump and we loaded them up.'

'Can you remember if it was a red van?' asked Harry.

'Why, yes, it was . . . Dark red, I think,' replied Barry.

Harry looked at Siri and they both raised their eyebrows.

'I offered him ten pounds for his trouble,' Barry went on. 'But he would only take five. Then he asked was there anything else. I said I'd think about it and he offered to call me the next day. That's why I gave him my card.'

'Did he call back?' said Charlie.

'No. Haven't seen him since,' Barry went on. 'Mind you, I expect he's been busy. I'd already given him the names of two or three folk living on their own who might be interested in some painting and decorating. I think I mentioned Mr and Mrs Jenkins down at Newlands Farm near Broxwood and Mrs Ogmore down Lyonshall way –'

'So this man didn't
seem strange at all?'
Harry interrupted.

'Not at all, or I
would never have
mentioned Major
Hart to him!'

'Who's Major Hart?' aked Siri.

'Old Major Hart lives over in Far Hall.
Do you know it? It's a big old house and
only him living there. It's near Sarnesfield.
Now there's a trusting man! Only the other
day he staggered into the shop with an old
oil painting. Poor chap. He's a bit doddery,
see? What did he want for it – just fifty

pounds! I told him not to be so daft – he could get thousands for it in a posh gallery!'

Barry chatted on, telling them about various people he knew. He said there wasn't one of them who didn't own some valuable furniture or some silver spoons. 'And of course, they like nothing better than to drop in and have a chat with me about them!' he smiled.

Harry looked at his friends and he could see that they were all thinking the same thing. Was the man who stole money from Mr Oakley going to play another trick on these people too? If they could warn Barry's friends about the thief then maybe they could catch him and stop him stealing from someone else.

Chapter 10

It was hard to get away from Barry

without seeming rude. But at last the four

children gathered outside on the green.

'He could talk your toenails off!' grinned Charlie. 'Still, at least now we've got a bit more to go on.'

'Important information!' agreed Siri.

'One thing's for sure,' said Harry. 'Red Van Man is on the look-out for people living on their own. He charms them and

finds ways of getting money off them. I bet he does a few little jobs for them – and then has a sneaky look round.'

'Yeah! For stuff to steal!' declared Charlie.

'Maybe,' said Jack, giving his knuckles an extra-loud crack. 'But he's cleverer than that. I bet he doesn't actually *steal* stuff. I reckon he just gets people to sell him things for next to nothing.'

'Exactly!' said Siri.

'OK. Next stop Sarnesfield,' said Harry, mounting his bike. 'Let's go and see if Major Thingy at Far Hall has had a visit from this crook!'

'Major *Hart*,' Siri reminded him. 'But don't forget that Barry mentioned plenty of other people living alone.'

'That's true,' agreed Charlie. '*And* Barry told Red Van Man where they all lived as well.'

'I have a suggestion!' said Siri. 'We spread out, and each visit a different house. When we hear something new about our crafty friend, we text each other. OK, GOGOs?'

'Yeah, but you'd need a memory like an elephant to remember all the names and places that Barry mentioned,' sighed Jack.

Siri blew on his knuckles and smiled.

'Call me Jumbo!' With that, he repeated every name Barry had mentioned and where they all lived.

Even Charlie was impressed. 'You should go on TV with your brain,' she laughed. 'So what's the plan now, Harry?'

Harry suggested Siri should check out Mr and Mrs Jenkins. Off he clanked. He sent Jack, with Charlie in tow, to find Mrs Ogmore.

Meanwhile, Harry powered off towards Sarnesfield and Far Hall. 'You all know what to do!' he called after the others. 'If you find our target, text "RVM" for Red Van Man and say where you are. Then the rest of us can back you up double-quick. If none of us has any luck, we meet at the G.O. at about three o'clock.'

Chapter 11

After twenty minutes, Harry was cycling through the gate to Far Hall. The drive leading up to the house was bumpy with deep potholes everywhere. Shrubs and bushes that had not been looked after for years grew almost right across it in places. Harry had to concentrate on not crashing into a bush or buckling his front wheel in a pothole.

That was why he didn't see the red van until he turned a corner and the drive suddenly opened out. It curved round a wide circular lawn and in the middle were the remains of a large stone fountain. The grass needed mowing and there was no water in the fountain. Beyond the grass circle, the van was parked just below six crumbling stone steps leading up to the

grand old front entrance of Far Hall.

Before Harry could dodge back behind a bush and hide, two men appeared. They were struggling through the open door with a heavy dark wooden chest. The man in work clothes leading the way backwards down the steps had his back to the drive.

But even from behind, his greasy white hair combed straight back gave him away.

It's him! thought Harry.

Meanwhile, the red-faced old gentleman in the brown tweed suit was struggling. 'Just a moment!' he panted. He lowered his end of the chest on to the top of the steps.

That was when he caught sight of Harry. 'You!' he shouted. 'What are you doing here? This is private property!'

The shock made Red Van Man miss his footing and sent him flying. He landed painfully on the

gravel on his backside. 'Watch what you're

doing!' he blurted out.

'I'm sorry,' gasped old Major Hart. 'It's

one of those horrible children from the

village. They turn up now and then to

throw stones at my windows.'

There was no time for Harry to waste.

He dropped his bike and dashed forward.

'I'm not here to throw stones! Don't listen to this man, Major! He's after your money! If he says that chest isn't worth much, he's lying to you.'

'How dare you?' roared the Major. 'You've no right to say things like that about people. You rude boy.'

Red Van Man scrambled to his feet and dusted himself down. His face snapped into a brilliant smile. 'Leave this to me, sir!' he said soothingly.

'You haven't let him have anything else, have you?' cried Harry.

The Major didn't say anything, but from the expression on his face it looked as though he probably had.

Red Van Man had heard enough. He

was face to face with Harry before the boy could make a move. He put his hands on Harry's shoulders and squeezed with a strong grip. 'What *is* the matter, son?' he said, pretending to smile.

Before Harry could yelp with pain, the man spun him round and poked him in the back. 'That's it. Off you go now.' His voice was gentle, but Harry felt as if he was being jabbed with sticks.

As Harry bent over to pick up his bike, a knee caught him from behind. It knocked him off balance so that he scraped his shin painfully against the raised pedal.

'Oh, I'm *so* sorry!' Red Van Man grinned.

To make sure that the Major thought it was an accident, Red Van Man called in a friendly voice, 'It's all a mistake, Major. The boy has got the wrong address. And now he's leaving.' He leaned down to get close to Harry's ear and whispered softly, 'Because if he doesn't, he's going to get his fancy wheels kicked in . . .'

Chapter 12

Red Van Man left Harry on the ground beside his bike and walked back towards the steps. 'Leave the chest to me now, Major,' he said. 'I can put that into the van myself.'

As he opened the back doors of the van, Harry slid his right hand into his jeans pocket. His trembling fingers found the small shiny cards on his key-ring. One of them felt warm and vibrated a little. He ran his thumb along the length of it. 'Nose-to-tail, I think,' he whispered and braced himself.

It was a good thing he did, because his first sight of the full-size spinosaurus was a shock. It reared up, huge and hissing, its long jaws snapping like a cracked whip. For a moment it glowed white-hot and then cooled to the colour of river-mud.

Yet the men took no notice. Harry thought surely they must see the monster and hear it. And couldn't they smell the stink of ancient swamp that came from it?

No. They gave no sign of noticing anything except an annoying boy. The beast turned sideways and flapped his

ragged sail – *WHOOMPH!* – and the doors
of the van slammed shut.

That got the attention of both the men
who nearly jumped out of their skins! Red
Van Man recovered himself first. 'Talk about
a freak gust of wind!' he exclaimed, and
stepped forward to open the doors again.

Another wave of the sail. Another mighty gale. Before Red Van Man could jump out of the way, the doors slammed together again, this time on his fingers. He screamed then danced about shaking his hands and tucking them under his armpits.

His smile was gone now. 'What are you playing at, boy?' he said angrily. He lunged at Harry, trying to grab him.

With a flick of his enormous snout, the invisible spinosaurus flipped the man through the air and sent him crashing against the side of the van.

As soon as he got his breath back, the man scrambled to his feet, pale with terror.

'He's not human!' he yelled to the Major. 'I'm out of here!' He leapt into the driver's seat, banged the door closed and locked it.

But as soon as he started the engine, several tonnes of dinosaur heaved the van towards the centre of the circle of grass at the speed of an express train. The van smashed into the fountain and tipped up.

High off the ground, the front wheels spun slowly. The back doors had not been closed properly and now that the van was tilted back, they swung open by themselves.

Wrapped in grey blankets, the Major's grandfather clock slid very gently on to the soft grass. It was followed by a large and rather splendid oil painting.

Red Van Man tried to escape, of course.
A savage swish from an armoured tail
with a hole through the tip stopped him. It
bashed a great dent in the door of the van
and trapped him inside.

Harry was nervous that something nastier might happen. 'Enough!' he said.

That seemed to do it. Spinosaurus obeyed him like a good dog and Harry stroked his scales. 'Tail-to-nose this time,' he muttered to himself.

Before you could say 'plasticated and pocketed', both things happened.

After that, Harry started bashing buttons on his mobile.

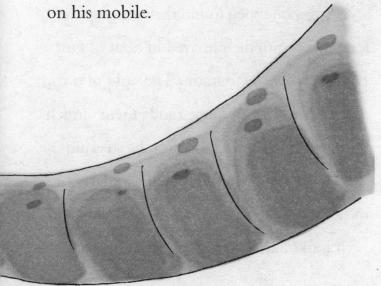

Chapter 13

By the time the rest of the gang was on the scene, so was Barry and so was Mr Oakley with his tractor.

One by one they found their way up the long drive until they arrived in front of Far Hall and saw the fountain. The sight of a van perched on it at an angle made them scratch their heads in wonder. Behind the steering wheel, Red Van Man sat quietly, looking rather sea-sick.

'It looks like a boat shipwrecked on a rock,'

said Siri with a smile.

In the mean time, Harry had explained to the poor dumbstruck Major why he and his friends had been after the man in the red van. He told him all about the dirty trick he had played on Mr Oakley.

When Barry turned up at Harry's request, he told the Major what he guessed was the real value of the things Red Van Man had nearly driven off with.

'An ancient chest like that must be worth thousands. The same goes for a two-hundred-year-old grandfather clock. And I told you before that you should ask a proper gallery to value your paintings for you. You mustn't go giving your valuable things away to strangers for a bit of pocket-money, Major!'

The Major looked crestfallen. 'You're quite right, I'm sure. But he talked so fast and he was such a friendly chap. I'm afraid I believed everything he said. I'm most grateful to you all, and especially to you, Harry, for coming to my rescue. You know, if you and your friends ever feel like making use of my tennis court, you'd be more than welcome.'

Harry, Jack, Charlie and Siri thought that would be brilliant. They would have thanked the Major properly, only just at that moment, Mr Oakley was doing something rather interesting. He was opening the bashed-in door on the driver's side of the van with his spade.

'Right, we're all set to winch the van

down! You can get out now,' yelled Mr Oakley over the noise of his tractor-engine.

Red Van Man's face was still pale with shock. Mr Oakley helped him climb down and then held out his open hand.

'There will be a small charge

for a tow to the nearest garage. And I can only take *folding money*. Is *folding money* all right with you?' Mr Oakley was enjoying this. 'It will be three hundred pounds plus a bit of money on top for my diesel. Then the Major will be wanting back the cash you took off him. Thank you.'

'Anything you say!' The man took a fat wallet out of his pocket and handed it to Mr Oakley. 'Take what you want. Just keep that kid away from me!' he said, glancing in terror at Harry.

Charlie turned to Harry. 'Wow! What did you *do* to him, Harry?' she gasped.

'And how on earth did the van end up in the air like that?' asked Jack.

'It's hard to explain,' said Harry. He

grinned and patted his pocket where
Spinosaurus was safely tucked away. 'Let's
just say I couldn't have done it without a
lot of back-up.'

Chapter 14

The rest of the weekend was very busy. Harry had to speak to the police about what had happened at Far Hall, and it looked like Red Van Man was in big trouble. By now the police had had lots of reports of people being tricked by a man fitting his description.

Harry got to school early on Monday morning. The only other kids who were around as he locked up his bike were Rocco Wiley and his mates.

'We've been looking for you, Dino-boy,'
sneered Rocco. 'You've been getting too big
for your boots, you have!' He pulled out his
lighter again and flicked it under the saddle
of Harry's bike.

'You shouldn't play with fire,' said Harry
quietly. His hand went to his front pocket.

His thumb moved. *Nose-to-tail*.

'Oh yeah? And who's going to stop me?' asked Rocco.

WHOOOOMPH!

From nowhere came a gust of wind so strong that it snatched the lighter from Rocco's hand and blew it away. The same gust ripped back the hoods he and his friends were wearing. It left them bare-headed and blinking with surprise.

'What's going on, Rocco?' said Philip Wells.

They all looked around, trying to work out what was happening.

But then Harry said something none of them would ever forget, though none of them ever talked about it to anyone.

What he said was: 'Spinosaurus . . . Show yourself!'

And for the first time in ages, Rocco and his friends had nothing to say.

Nobody could explain the change that came over Rocco Wiley that week.

'Quite amazing!' said the Head, Mrs Potts.

'I arrived on Monday morning to find that somebody had left Rocco and his friends dangling by their hoods from the coat-hooks outside my office. I expected them to tell me who did it, but they wouldn't say a word!'

On Wednesday, Rocco was seen at the supermarket pushing his baby brother in a shopping trolley.

'I can't believe it! Rocco? Helping his mum?' Jack said to Harry.

'And being nice to his baby brother!' added Charlie. 'What's going on?'

'It is a miracle!' was Siri's reply. 'Something very strange must have happened to change him so much.'

Harry smiled to himself. 'You can say that again.'